JUL 1997

DESIGNED BY RITA MARSHALL

CLAUDE LAPOINTE

OUT OF SIGHT!

CREATIVE EDITIONS

HARCOURT BRACE & COMPANY

OUT OF MIND!

FOR BEN, PHIL AND TOLA

*M*om said
we should play outside
today.

But it's so boring outside.
Nothing ever happens.

Let's play with
my new video game
instead.

See,
what did I tell you?

Nothing ever happens
outside.

Hey!
What's that over
there?

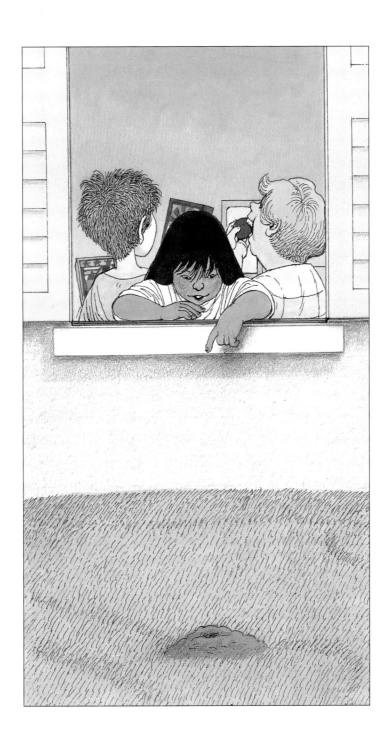

Permissions Department, Harcourt Brace & Company,
6277 Sea Harbor Drive, Orlando, Florida 32887-6777.
Creative Editions is an imprint of The Creative Company,
123 South Broad Street, Mankato, Minnesota 56001.
Library of Congress Cataloging-in-Publication Data
Lapointe, Claude. Out of sight, Out of mind / by Claude Lapointe.
Summary: As they play video games inside, children miss
out on a world of activity just outside their window.
ISBN 0-15-200956-6
[1. Nature—Fiction. 2. Animals—Fiction.] I. Title.
PZ7.L32027Ou 1995 [E]—dc20 94-38165
Printed in Italy
First edition A B C D E
Designed by Rita Marshall